Princess Charlotte
and the Enchanted Rose

By Vivian French
Illustrated by Sarah Gibb

ORCHARD BOOKS

The Royal Palace Academy
for the Preparation of Perfect Princesses

(Known to our students as "*The Princess Academy*")

OUR SCHOOL MOTTO:
*A Perfect Princess always thinks of others
before herself, and is kind, caring and truthful.*

Silver Towers offers a complete education for
Tiara Club princesses with emphasis on selected
outings. The curriculum includes:

Fans and Curtseys	*Problem Prime Ministers*
A visit to Witch Windlespin	*A visit to the Museum of Royal Life*
(Royal herbalist, healer and maker of magic potions)	*(Students will be well protected from the Poisoned Apple)*

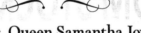

Our headteacher, Queen Samantha Joy, is present
at all times, and students are well looked after
by the school Fairy Godmother, Fairy Angora.

Our resident staff and visiting experts include:

LADY ALBINA MacSPLINTER *(School Secretary)*	QUEEN MOTHER MATILDA *(Etiquette, Posture and Poise)*
CROWN PRINCE DANDINO *(School Excursions)*	FAIRY G *(Head Fairy Godmother)*

We award tiara points to encourage our Tiara Club princesses towards the next level. All princesses who win enough points at Silver Towers will attend the Silver Ball, where they will be presented with their Silver Sashes.

Silver Sash Tiara Club princesses are invited to return to Ruby Mansions, our exclusive residence for Perfect Princesses, where they may continue their education at a higher level.

PLEASE NOTE:
Princesses are expected to arrive at the Academy with a *minimum* of:

TWENTY BALL GOWNS
(with all necessary hoops, petticoats, etc)

TWELVE DAY DRESSES

SEVEN GOWNS
suitable for garden parties, and other special day occasions

TWELVE TIARAS

DANCING SHOES
five pairs

VELVET SLIPPERS
three pairs

RIDING BOOTS
two pairs

Cloaks, muffs, stoles, gloves and other essential accessories as required

Good day, dear Tiara Club Princess.
Princess Charlotte sends you greetings!

Oh, it's no good. I don't think I'll EVER
be able to talk like a proper princess! But
I'm SO pleased you're coming to Silver
Towers at the Royal Palace Academy with
me and Katie, Daisy, Alice, Sophia and
Emily – it'll be SUCH fun! We'll float
about being TOTALLY Perfect Princesses,
and every day will be just perfect...

...although my first day wasn't
perfect AT ALL!

Chapter One

It was my first ever day at Silver Towers!

I was SO excited I could hardly breathe. I'd started packing weeks and weeks before, and I'd read the letter from the headteacher about a million times.

I kept pinching myself as our coach rattled along the road. I'd

Dear Princess Charlotte,

We look forward very much to welcoming you to Silver Towers, where you will continue your education at the Royal Palace Academy for the Preparation of Perfect Princesses. Please note that there will be a Royal Reception at 6.00pm, and dress accordingly.

With all good wishes,

Queen Samantha Joy

NB A map of Silver Towers is enclosed. Please make your way to the Grand Entrance on arrival.

been dreaming for so long that I was a proper Tiara Club princess at Silver Towers – and now I was nearly there.

My trunks were on the seat beside me, and I had a GORGEOUS new dress for the Royal Reception. It was pale violet silk, with the sweetest little matching shoes with real pearl buckles, so I really did feel ALMOST pretty when I wore it. (My hair's rather mousy, and my nose is VERY ordinary.)

And I was longing to see Katie, Daisy, Alice, Sophia and Emily. I'd missed them SO much over the holidays! Of course we'd sent loads of letters by Royal Messenger, but now we were going to be together again! When we finally turned in through the twirly silver gates I bounced from one side of

the coach to the other, trying
to see everything at once. The
silver towers were so romantic!
Even though it was a grey
day they were still shining,
and the tops reached right up to
the clouds.

We drove into a huge courtyard, and the coach stopped.

"Is this the place, Your Royal Highness?" the footman asked.

I fished around in my bag for the map – and it wasn't there. I'd forgotten it, even though Mum and Dad had reminded me about a hundred times before they went off on their Royal Tour. I could see an enormous doorway, though. That HAD to be the Grand Entrance, so I said, "Yes! This is it! Thank you!" The coachman piled my trunks by the step, and there I was – standing outside my new school.

*

RAT-A-TAT-TAT! I grabbed the knocker, and banged on the door with a flourish...and there wasn't any answer. And I suddenly noticed how quiet it was. Surely there should be other princesses arriving by now?

I began to feel just a teeny bit anxious. Could I be in the wrong place after all? I didn't quite see how I could be, because all the signs saying SILVER TOWERS: MAIN ENTRANCE had pointed to the courtyard where I was standing. I decided to go and check – just to be sure. I could see another archway in the wall beyond the front door, so I ran to look. It was beginning to rain, but I didn't take any notice.

OOOOPS!

I felt SO stupid. There was another sign pointing through the arch...and in the distance I could see rows of coaches.

They were standing outside a huge silver doorway that was SO amazing I realised I must have got out at the back door. Even though there was nobody to see, I went bright red. If ONLY I'd remembered the map!

I crept a little further through the arch, and something caught my eye – a rose! A real rose! It was lying in a muddy puddle, so I picked it up. And then I saw another, and another, and by the time I'd picked them all up I had a whole bunch. I was just wondering why they'd been thrown away when I heard the rumble of wheels behind me, and my heart jumped. Could it be my friends? It sounded like a big coach, and Sophia's coach was massive. I swung round to have a look – and I STARED!

The grandest coach I'd ever seen in my entire life was bowling towards me. It was so covered in glittering jewels I had to rub my eyes. It slowed down as it reached the archway, and I saw a snooty looking girl peering at me from the window. A voice said, "Look, Gruella! There's a HORRID dirty girl outside!" I had a quick glimpse of another sneering face, and it was weird – it was exactly the same!

And then they were through the arch and out the other side. I glared after them. They were so rude! I looked down at my lovely travelling dress. It was dripping wet, and COVERED in muddy splatters.

I nearly burst into tears. I'd thought being at Silver Towers was going to be fabulous and lovely, and it wasn't. It was absolutely HORRIBLE.

Chapter Two

I put the roses on the back doorstep, sat down next to my trunks, and stared at my sopping shoes. I could SO imagine how dreadful I'd look walking in through that massive silver doorway.

"CHARLOTTE! Whatever are you DOING?"

I knew that voice! I was SO pleased, I burst into tears – tears of happiness. A gigantic golden coach had stopped a little way away, and Sophia was hanging out of the window. Daisy, Emily and Katie were trying to peer round her, and they all looked really, really worried as they stared at me.

"It's all AWFUL!" I wailed. "I came to the wrong entrance and I'm completely soaked and my dress is ruined!"

The next minute they were running towards me.

"You POOR thing!" Emily said.

"You're wet right through!"

"Quick!" Katie caught my hand. "Get into the coach!"

Daisy grabbed my other hand, and we dashed through the rain.

We landed in Sophia's coach in a heap, and hugged each other...it was SO lovely to see them!

"Oh, look!" Katie began to giggle. "We're almost as wet as you are! But how did you get so muddy?"

"I was trying to find the front door," I said, "and this sparkly coach went right past me – it must have splashed me." I suddenly remembered the girls inside. "It was two princesses I've never seen before... I think they were twins."

"TWINS?" Emily's eyes lit up. "That'll be fun!"

"They didn't look like much fun," I said. "One twin said I was dirty."

27

Sophia looked horrified. "You mean they SAW you, and they didn't stop to help you?"

Daisy frowned. 'that's TERRIBLE. Princesses should always help people."

"It doesn't matter," I said. I was so happy to be with my friends

I didn't mind any more. "Do you know when Alice is arriving?"

"She WAS just behind us," Katie said. She scrambled onto the back seat, and peered through the window. "Yes! Here she is! Just coming into the courtyard! Oh – she's stopping!"

The next thing I knew, Alice was leaning out of the window of her coach, and Sophia was telling her how she'd found me. A second later Alice hopped in with us.

"Grandfather's telling his coachman to collect your luggage," she told me. "We'll arrive together... Goodness! You're soaked!"

"I know," I said. "And it's MY fault." And then a totally terrible thought struck me. Would

30

anybody ever believe we were princesses? Our hair was in rats' tails, our dresses were dripping, and our shoes were covered in mud. My stomach tied itself into knots. "What if they won't let us in?"

"They'll let Alice in," Daisy said. "She looks gorgeous!"

Daisy was right. Alice had a beautiful blue velvet dress on, and forget-me-not blue satin slippers.

Alice looked at us, and grinned a wicked grin. "Wait!" she

ordered, and before we could stop her she was outside, dancing in the rain. She didn't come back until she was just as wet as the rest of us.

"There!" she said. "If they don't want us, at least we can all be together! Look – Grandfather's coach is moving on. It's time to make our grand entrance at Silver Towers!"

Chapter Three

My heart was thumping as Sophia's coach drew up outside the massive front door. There was a red carpet walkway, and pageboys waiting with umbrellas. When they saw us getting out of the coach they had to try REALLY hard not to laugh, and that made Alice and Katie giggle – and a moment later we were all laughing. We hurried along the carpet and in through the door... It was awesome!

The hallway was ENORMOUS, and rows and rows of huge

glittery chandeliers positively dazzled us. We tried not to stare, but it was very hard not to. After the gloom of the rain outside it looked so sparkly and lovely, and it was deliciously warm too.

"Welcome – oh! Oh! OH! NEVER have I seen princesses arrive in such a state!"

The tall thin teacher standing by the door looked at us in the MOST despising way as she checked our names on her clipboard.

"You are all in Silver Rose Room. I shall order your trunks to be taken straight there, and you will change those DISGUSTING dresses. Queen Samantha Joy will be making her formal speech at the Royal Reception at six o'clock precisely, and you must NOT be late!"

And although Alice's lovely grandfather tried to explain what had happened, the teacher hooshed us away as if we were babies. She hardly let Alice kiss him goodbye and she kept tutting at us all the way up the white marble stairs.

"Now," she snapped as she opened a door and marched us through. "Be quick! And take SIX minus tiara points each!" The door slammed, and she was gone.

We sank down on a bed, and stared at each other.

"Minus tiara points?" I gasped.

"Didn't I tell you?" Alice said.

"When my big sis was here she got LOADS of minus points. She only just got enough to go on to Ruby Mansions." She picked up a pillow and thumped it. "Just before I left home she told me we'd have a huge surprise on our first day, but this is a horrible surprise!"

I looked at her, amazed. Alice is hardly ever cross.

"Maybe something good will happen soon," I said hopefully.

"Maybe." Alice still sounded fed-up. "It'll have to be VERY good to make up for minus tiara points."

I was beginning to feel uncomfortable. If I hadn't been so stupid, I'd have gone to the right door, and then I wouldn't have got wet, and then my friends wouldn't have got wet either...AND WE WOULDN't HAVE GOT ANY MINUS TIARA POINTS!

"I'm not sure if I'm going to like it here," Katie sighed, and Daisy nodded.

"We'd better get unpacked," Emily said gloomily, "or we'll be in even MORE trouble."

"At least we're all in the same dormitory." I was trying hard to be cheerful.

"But it's so plain!" Katie made a face. "Look! Washy pink walls, and b'rrrr! One tiny little rug!"

"It doesn't look like our old Rose Room," Daisy said wistfully.

Sophia suddenly sat up straighter. "Mmmm...I can *smell* roses!" she said.

We looked round – and there, on top of my luggage, were the roses I'd picked up and left on the step. The coachman must have thought I'd brought them with me.

"That's strange," I said as I looked at them. "They were all muddy when I found them."

Alice suddenly smiled. "Maybe they're magic!"

"They're gorgeous!" Sophia picked one up, and sniffed it. "Oh! That's just heavenly!"

And I had a totally brilliant idea.

"I'll share them round Rose Room!" I said. "Roses for the Rose Roomers – my VERY special friends!"

Chapter Four

It wasn't quite six o'clock when we hurried down the stairs. The dormitory looked SO much better by the time we shut the door; I'd put roses on everybody's bedside tables, and they made the room almost glow. We all felt better, too – even Alice was cheerful again. As I did my pearl buckles up I began to think maybe everything was going to be all right after all.

When we found the throne room, it was full of princesses. They were sitting in rows on white satin chairs, and we sneaked into the back as quietly as we could.

We could see Princess Freya, and Princess Jemima, and LOADS of our other friends...but there was no sign of horrible Princess Perfecta or beastly Princess Floreen. I heaved a sigh of relief. They'd been SO awful before!

And then I saw the twins. They were sitting on the other side of the aisle from us, and they were sneering as if they thought I was utterly TOTALLY horrible.

"Hey, Diamonde!" one said loudly. "It's that dirty girl again!"

But before the other twin could

answer, there was a fanfare of golden trumpets, and the most wonderful procession of beautifully dressed queens and kings paraded past us and up to the thrones in front of the velvet curtains.

"Wow!" I gasped – and then I clutched at Alice's arm. "LOOK!" I whispered. "It's Fairy G! AND Fairy Angora!"

And it was! Dear, DEAR Fairy G, our Fairy Godmother from before, was stumping along at the back of the procession. Beside her floated Fairy Angora, who we'd met just before we'd got into the Tiara Club. She was SO beautiful you could never forget her...even if she wasn't very good at magic spells.

"Fairy Angora looks dreadful!" Alice hissed in my ear.

She was right. Fairy Angora was very pale, and she kept blowing her nose.

I was about to say, "Maybe she's got a cold", but I suddenly saw our new headteacher frowning at us. She looked – I couldn't think of the right word, and then I thought, "MAGNIFICENT! But SO scary!"

"Good evening to you all," she said, and her voice was lovely... very deep and warm. I began to feel a tiny bit better, although she was still looking stern. "I am DELIGHTED to welcome such a splendid gathering of princesses to Silver Towers. I hope this will be a truly wonderful experience for each one of you, and that we will be able to congratulate you ALL on winning your Silver Sashes and moving on to Ruby Mansions when the time comes."

Queen Samantha Joy paused. "Unfortunately, I must bring a serious matter to your attention.

We are extremely pleased that we have been able to appoint Fairy Angora as the school Fairy Godmother – of course, some of you will have met her before.

Now, sometime between driving through the gates and arriving in school, she lost a very valuable and magic item. A search has taken place, but nothing had been found. I cannot imagine ANY of my princesses would be responsible, but I have to ask. Have any of you seen a bunch of enchanted roses?"

Chapter Five

I wanted to die. My heart was thumping so hard I thought everyone must have heard it. I felt SO awful.

I stood up, but before I could say a word the twins leapt into the aisle. One of them shouted, "WE saw someone sneaking around with a bunch of roses.

Didn't we, Gruella?"

Gruella nodded. "And we know who she is, don't we, Diamonde?"

The throne room was suddenly full of rustlings and murmurings. "It's HER!" Diamonde pointed straight at me.

And she and Gruella smirked triumphantly.

I looked at their grinning faces, and I RAN. The one thing I'm really good at is running, and I absolutely tore out of the throne room, up the stairs and into Rose Room. I seized the roses, and dashed back as fast as I could go. I was puffing hard, but I managed to walk steadily up to Queen Samantha Joy, and curtsey.

"Please," I said, "PLEASE excuse me. I found them in the mud." And then I curtsied again, and I only wobbled a very little bit. "I'm so VERY sorry—"

And I had to stop. If I'd said anything else I'd have burst into tears. I gulped loudly, and stared at my feet as I waited to be told I had to leave Silver Towers.

There was a moment of complete and utter silence, and then Fairy Angora spoke. "Would

the Princesses Gruella and Diamonde please come here?"

Sophia said afterwards that she just KNEW the twins thought they were going to be told how clever they were. They minced in between the rows of chairs as if they were collecting a million tiara points.

"Now," Fairy Angora said, and she sounded so sweet and kind I felt a zillion times worse. "Princess Charlotte, may I see the roses?"

I swallowed hard, and held them out.

It was SO odd! They looked even lovelier than they had before! Each rose had a sparkling silver dew drop deep in its velvet petals, and the scent almost made me dizzy. And I suddenly realised Alice had been right! They WERE magic.

Fairy Angora looked at them, and her smile was amazing.

62

I took a little sideways peep at
Fairy G, and she was smiling too.

"Aha," Fairy Angora said.

"Just as I thought." She took a
rose, and handed it to Gruella.
Gruella shrieked, and dropped it
at once.

"It's got HORRID thorns!" she squealed. "Don't TOUCH it, Diamonde!"

"Don't tell ME what to do, Gruella!" Diamonde snapped. She grabbed at the poor flower, and at once the petals lost their colour, and drooped miserably.

"You see?" Fairy Angora said gently. She tucked the rose back into the bunch I was still holding...and it was suddenly PERFECT again!

There was a loud "Ooooooh!" from everyone, even Queen Samantha Joy.

Fairy G beamed, and her eyes twinkled as she stepped forward.

"ENCHANTED ROSES ALWAYS KNOW WHEN SOMEONE HAS A TRULY KIND HEART," she boomed in her extraordinarily loud voice. "AND ALSO—" she gave Gruella and Diamonde a frosty stare, "WHEN THEY MEAN TO BE UNKIND."

And Gruella and Diamonde ZOOMED back to their chairs, blushing a horrible deep red.

"Well done, Fairy Godmother Angora! And well said, Fairy G!" Queen Samantha Joy began to laugh, and it was such a gorgeous deep chuckle I couldn't help laughing too. She bent down, and pinched my cheek.

"Poor little Charlotte! What a beginning to your time at Silver Towers! Why don't I give ten tiara points to everyone in Rose Room, to cheer you up."

And I could hardly believe it, but my magnificent new headteacher winked at me! "And now," she went on, "give Fairy Angora the roses, and run back to your seat. It's time we got ready for the Rose Petal Ball!"

Chapter Six

We'd never EVER guessed there was to be a ball that evening! We watched in amazement as Fairy Angora gently brushed the walls of the throne room with the enchanted roses, so they were instantly draped with palest pink satin covered in swathes of shimmering silver net.

Strings and strings of twinkly pink flower petal fairy lights looped themselves over the ceiling, and

music floated through the air in the most mysterious way. It was utterly and completely GORGEOUS!

Then Queen Samantha Joy began the dancing with Fairy G, and we couldn't help laughing as they sailed round the room together. They looked SO funny!

The grown-ups sat on the chairs and chatted...and Alice, Katie, Emily, Daisy, Sophia and I danced and DANCED until we could hardly keep our eyes open.

*

As we walked slowly up the stairs to our dormitory, Emily asked, "Was that the surprise your sister meant, Alice? The Rose Petal Ball?"

Alice yawned. "I don't know. It's been nothing but surprises ever since we got here."

I gave a little skip as we opened our door. "I LIKE surprises...well, I like the nice ones."

"That's good," Sophia said. She was in front of me, and I could see her eyes were wide. "Come and look!"

And we stared and stared.

On each of our beds was a heap of crimson velvet heart-shaped cushions...and a scatter of rose petals.

"Wow!" I gasped, "WOW!"

And as we snuggled down, I just knew that being at Silver Towers was going to be the happiest time in my life...and I'm SO glad you're here too.

What happens next?
Find out in

Princess Katie
and the Dancing Broom

Hello, and how are you?
Thank you SO much for being at
Silver Towers with us...
Oh! You do know who we are, don't you?
I'm Princess Katie, and I share the
Silver Rose Room with the
Princesses Charlotte, Alice, Emily,
Daisy and Sophia. We're all trying
really hard to win our Silver Sashes - but
it's hard work getting
Tiara Points, especially when
those HORRIBLE twins are around...

Check out

website at:

www.tiaraclub.co.uk

You'll find Perfect Princess games and fun
things to do, as well as news on the Tiara
Club and all your favourite princesses!

Win a Tiara Club
Perfect Princess Prize!

Look for the secret word in mirror writing hidden in a tiara in each of the Tiara Club books. Each book has one word. Put together the six words from books **7** to **12** to make a special Perfect Princess sentence, then send it to us together with 20 words or more on why you like the Tiara Club books. Each month, we will put the correct entries in a draw and one lucky reader will receive a magical Perfect Princess prize!

Send your Perfect Princess sentence, your name and your address on a postcard to:
The Tiara Club Competition,
Orchard Books, 338 Euston Road,
London, NW1 3BH

Australian readers should write to:
Hachette Children's Books,
Level 17/207 Kent Street, Sydney, NSW 2000.

Only one entry per child.
Final draw: 31 August 2007

By Vivian French
Illustrated by Sarah Gibb

PRINCESS CHARLOTTE
AND THE BIRTHDAY BALL   ISBN   1 84362 863 5

PRINCESS KATIE
AND THE SILVER PONY   ISBN   1 84362 860 0

PRINCESS DAISY
AND THE DAZZLING DRAGON   ISBN   1 84362 864 3

PRINCESS ALICE
AND THE MAGICAL MIRROR   ISBN   1 84362 861 9

PRINCESS SOPHIA
AND THE SPARKLING SURPRISE   ISBN   1 84362 862 7

PRINCESS EMILY
AND THE BEAUTIFUL FAIRY   ISBN   1 84362 859 7

The Tiara Club at Silver Towers

PRINCESS CHARLOTTE
AND THE ENCHANTED ROSE   ISBN   1 84616 195 9

PRINCESS KATIE
AND THE DANCING BROOM   ISBN   1 84616 196 7

PRINCESS DAISY
AND THE MAGICAL MERRY-GO-ROUND   ISBN   1 84616 197 5

PRINCESS ALICE
AND THE CRYSTAL SLIPPER   ISBN   1 84616 198 3

PRINCESS SOPHIA
AND THE PRINCE'S PARTY   ISBN   1 84616 199 1

PRINCESS EMILY
AND THE WISHING STAR   ISBN   1 84616 200 9

All priced at £3.99.

The Tiara Club books are available from all good bookshops, or can be ordered direct
from the publisher: Orchard Books, PO BOX 29, Douglas IM99 1BQ.

Credit card orders please telephone 01624 836000 or fax 01624 837033 or visit our
Internet site: www.wattspub.co.uk or e-mail: bookshop@enterprise.net for details.

To order please quote title, author, ISBN and your full name and address.

Cheques and postal orders should be made payable to "Bookpost plc.©

Postage and packing is FREE within the UK

(overseas customers should add £2.00 per book).

Prices and availability are subject to change.